DC SUPER-PETS!™

DC Super-Pets! Origin Stories are published by
Stone Arch Books
A Capstone Imprint
1710 Roe Crest Drive
North Mankato, Minnesota 56003
www.mycapstone.com

STAR38955

Cataloging-in-Publication Data is available at the Library of Congress website.
ISBN: 978-1-4965-5139-9 (library binding)
ISBN: 978-1-4965-5143-6 (paperback)
ISBN: 978-1-4965-5147-4 (eBook)

Summary: Even Superman needs a loyal sidekick. But how did Krypto the Super-Dog become
the Man of Steel's best friend? Discover the origin of this superpowered Super-Pet in the this
action-packed, POW!-WHAM!-BOOM! book for early readers.

Designed by Bob Lentz

Printed and bound in the United States of America.
010372F17

KRYPTO!

The Origin of Superman's Dog

by Michael Dahl
illustrated by Art Baltazar
Superman created by Jerry Siegel and Joe Shuster
by special arrangement with the Jerry Siegel Family

STONE ARCH BOOKS
a capstone imprint

EVERY SUPER HERO NEEDS A
SUPER-PET!

Even Superman!
In this origin story, discover
how Krypto the Super-Dog
became the Man of Steel's
best friend . . .

Trillions of miles from Earth, on the planet Krypton, live two happy parents.

They have a beloved puppy and a new baby boy named Kal-El.

Little do they know, their son will become the World's Greatest Super Hero — **Superman!**

One day, Kal-El's scientist father, Jor-El, discovers that Krypton will soon explode.

His inventions measure rumblings deep within the planet.

RUUUU-UU-UUMMM-BLE!

"I must warn the other scientists right away!" Jor-El exclaims.

Krypton's other scientists do not believe his warnings.

Jor-El and his wife, Lara, make plans for a rocket ship that will save their family.

"We must test smaller rockets first," Jor-El tells his wife.

"But who will make the test flights?" Lara wonders.

Jor-El and Lara decide to use the family puppy, Krypto.

Although he's little, Krypto is big-time brave and eager to help.

"Ruff! Ruff!" He barks farewell as the tiny rocket launches into space.

ZWOOOOSH!

Then the quakes grow stronger. Jor-El doesn't have time to build a larger ship.

He and Lara place baby Kal-El into another small rocket.

The boy thinks of his puppy, Krypto, and remembers to be brave.

Kal-El soars into space!

The planet Krypton suddenly explodes!

Farther out among the stars, Krypto's rocket hits a meteor.

His ship hurtles off course, and the brave bowwow falls into a deep sleep.

Some time later, baby Kal-El's rocket crash-lands on Earth. KA-BLAM!

He is adopted by a kind couple, Jonathan and Martha Kent, and becomes known as their son, Clark.

Soon, Clark discovers he has superpowers. But he keeps them a secret.

Only his parents know that he is the hero **Superman!**

Years later, Clark and his father visit the local grocery store.

Suddenly, a robber rushes in and steals the store's money.

When the robber runs outside, Clark is about to change into Superman.

Then suddenly, a white dog appears and snatches the robber in his jaws!

The superpowered pup drops the crook and the loot on the store's doorstep.

Then he speeds away like a rocket.

"Something's familiar about that crafty canine," Clark thinks.

Using his X-ray vision, Clark tracks down the dog.

The powerful pooch is hiding behind a rocket that has crash-landed nearby. Its controls are written in the same language found in Superman's old spaceship.

The ship came from his home planet, Krypton!

"Now I remember!" Superman says.

Years after hitting the meteor, his furry friend has finally arrived safely on Earth.

"Krypto!" Superman shouts with glee.

"Ruff! Ruff!" Krypto barks happily at the sight of his old friend.

Soon after, Superman makes the dog a special cape and collar out of materials from his rocket.

Krypto is his pet once again!

Krypto shares many of the same powers as his master, including flight, X-ray vision, super-hearing, and super-strength.

He also shares Superman's great
weakness: **Kryptonite!**

Green Kryptonite robs both heroes of
their powers. Red Kryptonite affects them
in other, strange ways.

One day, Superman touches Red Kryptonite and develops deadly vision. Whatever he looks at turns into diamonds!

To protect others, Superman refuses to open his eyes.

Krypto serves as Superman's seeing-eye dog until his vision returns.

"Good old Krypto!" Superman thanks him.

From then on, Krypto fights side by side with Superman as his first and best companion.

Eventually, Clark moves to the busy city
of Metropolis and becomes a reporter.

Meanwhile, Krypto flies into outer
space, hungry for adventure.

He joins an exciting band of dog heroes:
the Space Canine Patrol Agents!

Together, they battle for justice.
They defend the weak and defeat evil
throughout the universe.

Back on Earth, Superman works on a special project — a water pipeline that will bring water to thousands who live in the desert.

Superman uses his super-strength to plow through solid rock, digging a trench for the pipeline.

His hands carve through thick granite.

Suddenly, the Man of Steel rams into a chunk of buried Kryptonite!

Superman's powers slowly drain away. No one is around to rescue him!

But Krypto is on his way back to Earth!

With his super-vision, he spies his former master next to the Kryptonite.

ZOOOOM!

The powerful pooch rockets down to one end of the trench.

He huffs and puffs.

WHOOOSH! His super-breath blows through the trench and blasts the Kryptonite out the other end.

Superman is saved!

"Krypto! You were my pet before I was Superman!" cries out the Man of Steel. **"But now you're a Super-Pet!"**

Once again, the two friends are united.

And once again, the world is patrolled and protected by the greatest hero team of all — Superman and his dog, Krypto!

"Ruff! Ruff!"

KRYPTO!

REAL NAME:
Krypto

SPECIES:
Super-dog

BIRTHPLACE:
Krypton

HEIGHT:
22.5 inches

WEIGHT:
64 pounds

Super Hero Owner:
SUPERMAN

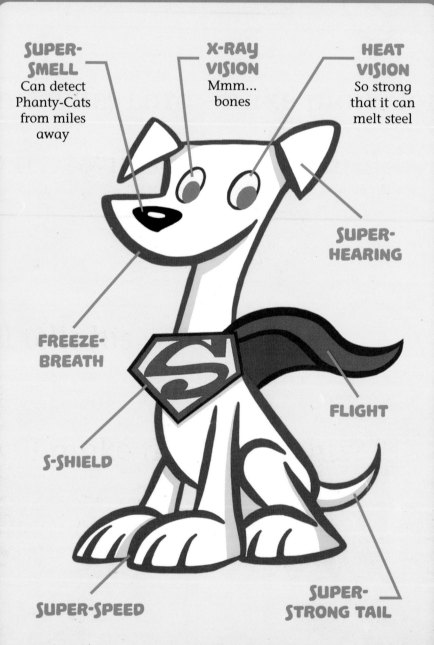

SUPER-SMELL
Can detect Phanty-Cats from miles away

X-RAY VISION
Mmm... bones

HEAT VISION
So strong that it can melt steel

SUPER-HEARING

FREEZE-BREATH

S-SHIELD

FLIGHT

SUPER-SPEED

SUPER-STRONG TAIL

HERO PET PALS!

BEPPO

Super Hero Owner:
SUPERMAN

SUPER-TURTLE

Super Hero Owner:
SUPERMAN

FUZZY

Super Hero Owner:
SUPERBOY

COMET

Super Hero Owner:
SUPERGIRL

STREAKY

Super Hero Owner:
SUPERGIRL

SCOOP

Owner:
LOIS LANE

VILLAIN PET FOES!

BIZARRO KRYPTO

Super-Villain Owner:
BIZARRO

DESTRUCTO

Super-Villain Owner:
LEX LUTHOR

BRAINIAC BUG

Super-Villain Owner:
BRAINIAC

DRIBODOD

Super-Villain Owner:
MR. MXYZPTLK

OMEGAN

Super-Villain Owner:
DARKSEID

BANJO

Super-Villain Owner:
TOYMAN

KRYPTO JOKES!

What is a dog's favorite dessert?
Pup-cakes!

What do you get when you cross a dog and an airplane?
A jet setter!

Why is a tree like a big dog?
They both have a lot of bark!

GLOSSARY!

companion (kuhm-PAN-yuhn)—a friend or someone to spend time with

justice (JUHSS-tiss)—the system of laws in a country

Krypton (KRIP-tohn)—Superman and Krypto's home planet, which was destroyed

Kryptonite (KRIP-toh-nite)—a radioactive rock from Krypton that weakens Superman and Krypto

meteor (MEE-tee-ur)—a piece of rock from space that enters Earth's atmosphere, burns, and forms a streak of light in the sky

universe (YOO-nuh-vurss)—the Earth, the planets, the stars, and all things that exist in space

READ THEM ALL!

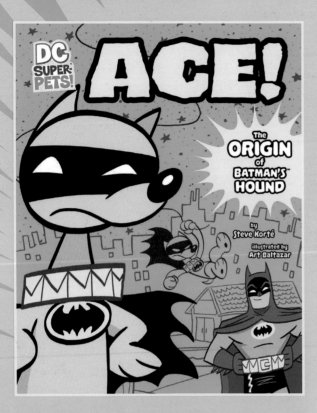

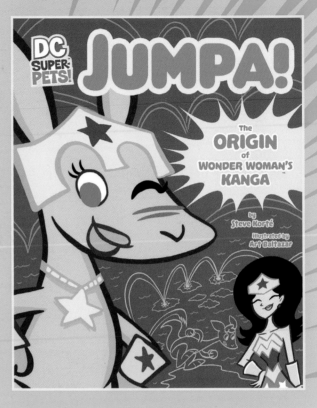

MORE KRYPTO STORIES!

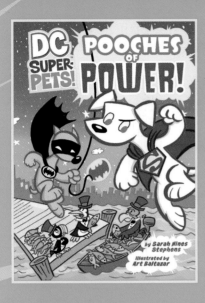

ALL ABOUT YOUR FAVORITE SUPER-PETS!

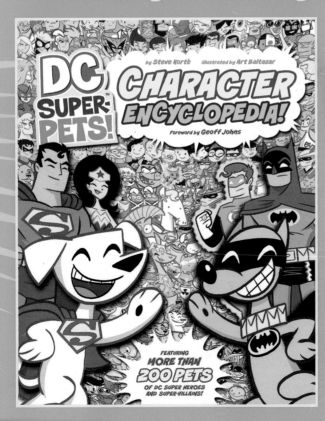

AUTHOR!

Michael Dahl is the prolific author of more than 200 books for children and young adults, including the DC Super-Pets chapter book *The Fantastic Flexy Frog.* He has won the AEP Distinguished Achievement Award three times for his nonfiction, a Teachers' Choice Award from *Learning* magazine, and a Seal of Excellence from the Creative Child Awards. He currently lives in Minneapolis, Minnesota in a haunted house.

ILLUSTRATOR!

Famous cartoonist Art Baltazar is the creative force behind *The New York Times* bestselling, Eisner Award-winning DC Comics' Tiny Titans; co-writer for Billy Batson and the Magic of Shazam, Young Justice, Green Lantern Animated (Comic); and artist/co-writer for the awesome Tiny Titans/Little Archie crossover, Superman Family Adventures, Super Powers, and Itty Bitty Hellboy! Art is one of the founders of Aw Yeah Comics comic shop and the ongoing comic series! Aw yeah, living the dream! He stays home and draws comics and never has to leave the house! He lives with his lovely wife, Rose, sons Sonny and Gordon, and daughter Audrey! AW YEAH MAN! Visit him at www.artbaltazar.com